ILLINOIS PRAIRIE DPL

D1088185

Babar characters TM & © 1991 L. de Brunhoff
All rights reserved

Based on the animated series "Babar"
A Nelvana-Ellipse Presentation
a Nelvana Production in Association with The Clifford Ross Company, Ltd
Based on characters created
by Jean and Laurent de Brunhoff
Based on a story by B. P. Nichols
Image adaptation by Van Gool-Lefèvre-Loiseaux
Produced by Twin Books U.K. Ltd, London
Published by Binky Books
An Imprint of Grange Books Ltd
The Grange
Grange Yard
London SE1 3AG
ISBN 1-85627-099-8
This edition published in 1992
Printed and bound in Hong Kong

BABAR

The Best Present
in the World

ILLINOIS PRAIRIE DISTRICT LIBRARY

106171

It was Queen Celeste's birthday, and Babar was planning a big party with his loyal advisors, Pompadour and General Cornelius.

"May I recommend the linen napkins, Sire?" suggested Pompadour. He bowed so deeply that his monocle almost fell off.

"Personally," said Cornelius, "*I* prefer the silk napkins – for the shining example that Queen Celeste is to us all."

Babar didn't know how to decide without offending either of his friends. Luckily, the children interrupted the debate.

"Papa!" demanded Pom, Flora, and Alexander. "What shall we get Mama for her birthday? It must be something very special."

"Hmmmm," said Babar, joining the children. "This reminds me of the time I learned something about gift-giving. It was the morning of the Old Lady's birthday, and, like you, we wanted to give her the best present ever. Cousin Alexander and Zephir were looking at the huge pile of presents in the hall, wondering what was in each package . . ."

"I hope," said Zephir, "that these aren't dull, ordinary old presents. I think we should give her something rare and wonderful. Like an electric rocking chair. Or a four-banana toaster – for when I come over. Or a Weeping Wonder Bird feather for her hat!"

"That's rare!" cried Barbar. "In fact, it's perfectly wonderful. And wonderfully perfect!"

"Now, wait a minute, please," protested Zephir. "I was only kidding. The Weeping Wonder Bird lives way up Way Up Peak."

"We can find it!" said Babar. "Let's go before the party starts!"

Grumbling, Zephir followed Babar out of the palace.

In another palace nearby, Rataxes, the rhinoceros King, was using his Babar tees for golfing practice.

"Five!" he shouted, taking a wild swing.

"I believe that's 'Fore,' Your Highness," suggested his advisor, Basil, from the sidelines.

"Never mind, Basil," said Rataxes. He went over to the wall where all his Babar tees were stuck. "I've got that Babar right where I want him. I can tell we'll play a good round this afternoon."

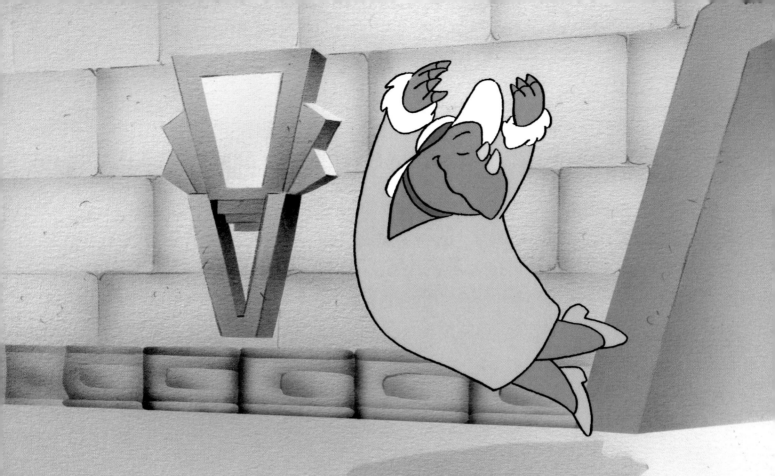

Just then, Lady Rataxes danced into the room and struck a ballet pose. "I have just heard," she announced, "that Babar has set out for Way Up Peak to get a Weeping Wonder Bird feather for the Old Lady's birthday."

Leaping into Rataxes' arms, she continued, "It just shows how much Barbar loves her. More than *some* love *others*."

"But, but – " spluttered Rataxes. "It's not your birthday or any other special day."

"That's not the point," sighed Lady Rataxes romantically. "If you were to get *me* such a feather, it would show the whole world how much you love me."

Rataxes hated to give up his golf game, but he really had no choice.

"Never mind," he grumbled to Basil. "I'll just golf my way up Way Up Peak."

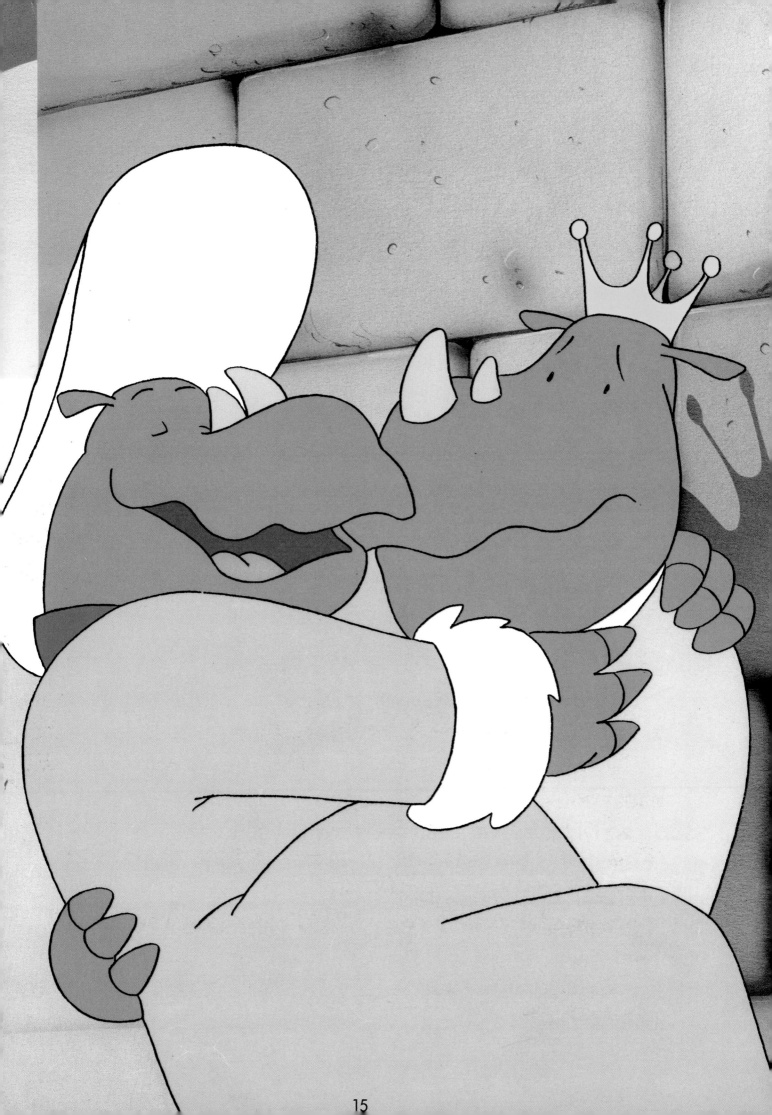

Babar and Zephir were struggling up a cliff when they spotted Rataxes and Basil halfway up the Peak.

"Uh-oh," said Zephir. "It looks like someone else is after the Weeping Wonder Bird feather."

"Never mind," said Babar. "Rataxes isn't going to stop us, and neither is Way Up Peak. Once we cross that river over there, we'll be very close."

They started to pole across the river on a floating log, but suddenly, Zephir was snatched from the log by a crocodile!

Babar dived in after Zephir, who bobbed to the surface. Then the crocodile dived after both of them!

"What'll we do?" yelled Zephir. "Beg for mercy? Sing him a song?"

"A song?" asked the crocodile in a deep voice. "I *love* music." He sat up in the water to listen.

In trembling voices, Babar and Zephir made up a little song about the day's adventures, and danced to it as well.

"Lovely," sighed the crocodile. Then he picked up the two friends in his tail and got them to sing it all over again. They made up a second verse and ended with a rousing finale: "Wa up on Way Up Peak."

By this time, the crocodile had fallen asleep. His tail came to rest on the riverbank.

"Hooray!" cried Babar and Zephir, leaping off the crocodile's tail. They ran on up the steep hillside.

While the crocodile was still napping underwater, Rataxes hit a golf ball onto his back. "It's a water trap," he said to Basil, preparing to tee off again.

Just then, the crocodile rose from the water to his full length. "Sing me a song!" he demanded.

Rataxes and Basil stared at him with their teeth chattering. Then Rataxes got angry. "We don't have time for that!" he said impatiently. "We're playing through."

The crocodile roared with rage, and the frightened rhinos dove into the water. The three of them fought until Rataxes' favorite golf club was completely bent out of shape. Then the crocodile sent them flying with a powerful swipe of his tail.

"Fore!" shouted Basil.

"Help!" cried Rataxes.

Meanwhile, Babar and Zephir had finally reached the top of the Peak. Sure enough, the Weeping Wonder Bird was sitting on her nest and crying as if her heart would break.

"Visitors!" she wailed, when she saw Babar and Zephir. "And I must look a fright! Oh, boo hoo!"

"Don't cry," said Babar. "We didn't mean to scare you."

"But I'm crying because I'm happy," sobbed the Weeping Wonder Bird.

"I have so few visitors up here," she explained, blowing her nose. "Please, take a seat." Then she burst out crying again. "But I have no chairs!" she wailed. "Oh, what is the matter with me?"

ILLINOIS PRAIRIE DISTRICT LIBRARY 106171

"That's okay," said Babar soothingly. "We really can't stay. But we came to see you because we want to give a special friend the best present in the world."

"You must mean my tail feather," sniffed the Weeping Wonder Bird. (And, indeed, it was a beautiful feather, sparkling gold all over and curled at the top.)

"Take it," said the bird, plucking out the feather. "It's little enough to give such well-mannered guests. I can always grow a new one. In fact, there's not much else to do up here."

"How can we thank you?" said Babar gratefully. "We will come and visit you again very soon."

"That would be lovely," sobbed the bird, waving her handkerchief after them. But no sooner had they gone than she had more visitors!

"Where's the feather?" demanded Rataxes rudely, as Basil stared at the crying bird.

"Even a bore and a bully could ask nicely," she replied, sniffing. "But you're too late anyway. I just gave my last feather to a very nice elephant and his monkey friend."

"Let's go, Basil!" said Rataxes, sliding back down the cliff. They soon picked up the trail of Babar and Zephir, who had put the golden feather into a bag.

Rataxes sneaked up behind Zephir and grabbed the bag. "I'll take that!" he said triumphantly.

"Oh, no, you won't!" cried Babar, spinning around to chase Rataxes.

"We stole it fair and square!" said the rhino King, as he and Basil seized some trailing vines and swung away through the trees.

"Quick, Zephir!" shouted Babar. The agile monkey grabbed another vine and took off in pursuit, followed by Babar. There was a wild chase through the treetops. The feather was captured and recaptured half a dozen times. Then – disaster struck. Babar fell from the vine into a pool of quicksand! He was sinking fast.

Zephir called, "Don't struggle – you'll only sink faster! I'm coming!"

He tried to reach Babar's trunk from an overhead branch, but he was inches short of his friend. Then he fell into the quicksand too!

Meanwhile, Rataxes stood on the bank and argued with himself about whether or not he should rescue Babar.

"After all," he muttered, "Babar got himself into this. It's the law of the jungle. Would he save *me* if it were the other way around?"

In his heart, Rataxes knew that the answer was yes.

"Oh, all *right*," he grumble
reaching for the branch. "Bas
pull on that vine!" Rataxes
scrambled onto the lowered
branch and fished Babar out
with his golf club. Zephir clur
to his tail.

Just as Babar flew free, Rataxes got his foot caught in the vine and fell head-first from the branch. "This is what I get for being a softy!" he spluttered, hanging upside-down. "I hope this doesn't get around. I'll never live it down."

"Basil, *h-e-l-l-p-p*!" shouted Rataxes. But it was Babar who came running to his assistance, calling:

"You saved my life, Rataxes! You'll be the hero of all Celesteville!"

Zephir added, "Elephant mothers will bring their children to see the rhino who saved their King!"

"Please, Babar," begged Rataxes. "Say nothing about this. My reputation will be ruined. Here!" he added, handing over the feather. "Take it. But promise you'll never tell anyone I rescued you."

"Well, if you insist," said Babar. Giggling, Zephir promised, "Don't worry Rataxes. We won't tell anyone that you're really a softy."

Rataxes gritted his teeth as they left.

When Babar and Zephir arrived at the party, they gave the feather to the Old Lady. But now it was all bedraggled from their adventures. Babar said sadly, "We wanted to give you the best present in the world."

"A Weeping Wonder Bird feather!" she exclaimed. "You and Zephir went all the way up Way Up Peak for me?"

"But it's ruined," said Babar.

"No, it isn't," she replied. "The lovely thought behind it makes it beautiful to me."

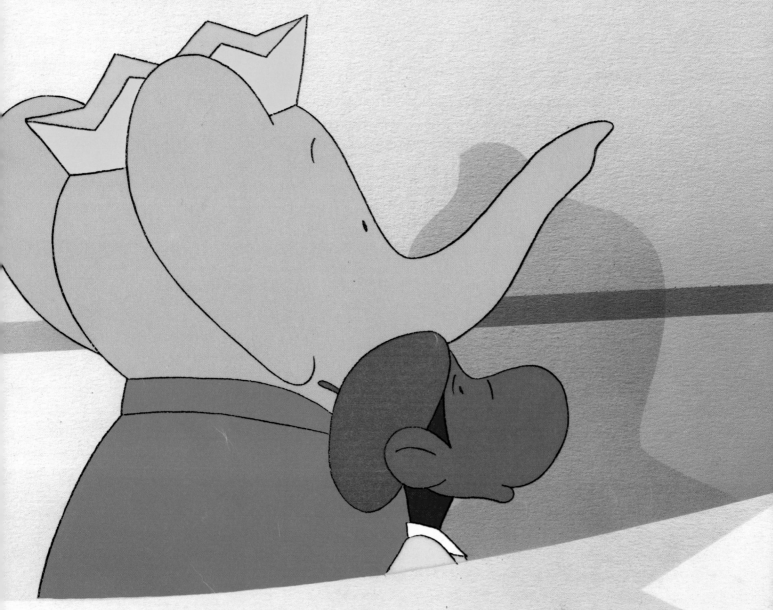

"And so, children," concluded Babar, "that's how I found out that the best presents are those that come from the heart."

"What a lovely story, Papa," said Flora. Pom and Alexander nodded agreement.

"And now," said Babar, "let's go find a rare and wonderful present for your mother. What do you say to – a toaster?"

"You're funny, Papa," laughed the children, running out to play.